For Ella,
with love from Mandy x

First published in the United Kingdom in 2004
by Chrysalis Children's Books, an imprint of Chrysalis Books Group plc
The Chrysalis Building, Bramley Road, London W10 6SP
This paperback edition first published in 2005

Text and illustrations copyright © 2004 Mandy Stanley

BRITISH LIBRARY CATALOGUING-IN-PUBLICATION DATA
A catalogue record for this book is available from the British Library.

ISBN 1 85602 487 3 (hardback)
ISBN 1 84458 054 7 (paperback)
Printed in China

Tilly

Who Tickled
Tilly?

Mandy Stanley

Chrysalis Children's Books

Tilly was snoozing in the sun
when something happened!

"Hey! What was that?

Someone tickled
my nose.

Ahhhh... ah...

Atishooo!"

She saw Crow.
"Did you tickle my nose?"

"No, I'm much too busy.
Perhaps it was Frog."

Tilly found Frog.
"Was it you, did you tickle my nose?"

Frog splashed into the water
and said in a bubbly voice,

"oh no... no... no...

It wasn't me!"

"Who tickled me?" thought Tilly.
The baby rabbits were nearby.

"Babies, did you tickle my nose when I was sleeping?"

The babies shook their heads and all together said, "No!"

Tilly wondered if she had been
dreaming. "I was snoozing -
perhaps nobody tickled me at all."

"I'm tired. I'll close my eyes for a nap."
At that moment – it happened again!

Tilly jumped up. Nobody was there. This was a mystery.

She slowly looked around. "A-ha... I know, it was Piglet!"

Piglet was having fun in the mud.

Tilly squelched through
the mud to reach Piglet.
"I know it was him, he's
always playing tricks."

Piglet was surprised.
"I didn't do anything... Oink, but I know,
oink, who did, oink!"

"Who?" bleated Tilly.

Piglet squealed and told Tilly
to look behind her.
Tilly looked around but at first
she couldn't see anyone.

Then something amazing appeared
from the poppies...

It was a beautiful, shimmering dragonfly.
Tilly raced after it.
She called out, "Was it you?"
But the dragonfly soared high

up into the bright blue sky...

...then swooped down to flutter
above Tilly's head.

"Yes, it was me!" he giggled.
"Do you want to play?"

So Tilly and the dragonfly and all the other
animals played together in the sunshine.